Copyright © 2023 by Publisher for w
All rights reserved. No part of this
transmitted in any form or by any me;
including photocopying, recording, or by any information storage and
retrieval system, without permission in writing from the publisher.

This is a work of fiction. Names, characters, places, and incidents
either are the product of the author's imagination or are used fictitiously.
Any resemblance to actual events, locales, or persons, living or dead, is
entirely coincidental.

Table of Contents

The Game of Hearts, Spies & Power
By
Mohd Anas Ali

Chapter 1: The Assignment

The year is 2042. The world is in a state of political and economic turmoil. The United States and China are locked in a Cold War, and both sides are engaged in a covert war of espionage.

In this world, there is a spy named Alex. Alex is a brilliant and resourceful agent who works for the CIA. He is tasked with infiltrating the Chinese government and stealing their secrets.

Alex's mission takes him to China, where he poses as a businessman. He quickly establishes himself in the Chinese elite, and he begins to gather information about the Chinese government's plans.

One day, Alex learns that the Chinese government is developing a new weapon that could change the balance of power in the world. He knows that he must stop them, but he also knows that it will be a dangerous mission.

Chapter 2: The Infiltration

Alex begins his infiltration of the Chinese government by attending a high-level conference on nuclear weapons. He meets with key Chinese officials and learns more about the new weapon that they are developing.

Alex also begins to build relationships with Chinese scientists and engineers. He learns that they are working on a new type of nuclear weapon that is much more powerful than anything that has been created before.

Alex knows that he must stop the Chinese government from developing this new weapon, but he also knows that he needs more information. He decides to go undercover and work as a scientist at the Chinese nuclear weapons facility.

Chapter 3: The Discovery

Alex's undercover work at the Chinese nuclear weapons facility is going well. He has gained the trust of his colleagues and he has learned a lot about the new weapon that they are developing.

One day, Alex makes a startling discovery. He learns that the Chinese government is planning to use the new weapon to attack the United

States. Alex knows that he must stop them, but he also knows that he is in danger.

Alex escapes from the Chinese nuclear weapons facility with the plans for the new weapon. He then makes his way back to the United States, where he delivers the plans to the CIA.

Chapter 4: The Chase

The Chinese government is furious that Alex has stolen the plans for their new weapon. They send their best agents to track him down and bring him back to China.

Alex is on the run. He is pursued by Chinese agents all over the world. He must use all of his skills and resources to stay ahead of them and protect the plans for the new weapon.

Alex eventually makes it back to the United States, but the Chinese government is not giving up. They continue to send agents after him, and they are determined to get the plans back.

Chapter 5: The Rescue

The Chinese government is closing in on Alex. They know that he is in the United States, and they are determined to find him.

The CIA knows that Alex is in danger, and they send a team to rescue him. The team tracks Alex down and helps him to escape.

Alex is safe, but the war between the United States and China is not over. The Chinese government will stop at nothing to get the plans back, and Alex must be prepared for the next battle.

STORY -I
War for the Power

Chapter 1: The Assignment

The year is 2042. The world is in a state of political and economic turmoil. The United States and China are locked in a Cold War, and both sides are engaged in a covert war of espionage.

In this world, there is a spy named Alex. Alex is a brilliant and resourceful agent who works for the CIA. He is tasked with infiltrating the Chinese government and stealing their secrets.

Alex's mission takes him to China, where he poses as a businessman. He quickly establishes himself in the Chinese elite, and he begins to gather information about the Chinese government's plans.

One day, Alex learns that the Chinese government is developing a new weapon that could change the balance of power in the world. He knows that he must stop them, but he also knows that it will be a dangerous mission.

The Meeting

Alex is sitting in a meeting room at the CIA headquarters in Langley, Virginia. He is facing a panel of senior CIA officials, including the Director of the CIA.

The Director is a tall, thin man with a stern look on his face. He speaks in a low, raspy voice.

"Alex," the Director says, "we have a very important mission for you. We need you to go to China and infiltrate the Chinese government. We believe that they are developing a new weapon that could change the balance of power in the world. We need you to stop them."

Alex nods. "I understand," he says. "I'm ready for the mission."

The Director hands Alex a file. "This file contains everything you need to know about the mission," he says. "Study it carefully and then we'll talk again tomorrow."

Alex takes the file and leaves the meeting room. He goes to his office and starts to read the file. The file contains a lot of information about the Chinese government, including their plans for the new weapon. Alex reads the file carefully, and he begins to formulate a plan for his mission.

The Plan

Alex's plan is to pose as a businessman who is interested in investing in China. He will use this cover to gain access to the Chinese government and to start gathering information about the new weapon. Once he has enough information, he will steal the plans for the weapon and bring them back to the CIA.

Alex knows that his mission will be dangerous. The Chinese government is not going to take kindly to someone who is trying to steal their secrets. Alex will need to use all of his skills and resources to stay alive and to complete his mission.

The Preparation

Alex spends the next few days preparing for his mission. He studies the file that the Director gave him, and he trains in martial arts and weapons. He also learns about Chinese culture and customs.

On the day of his mission, Alex is confident that he is ready. He boards a plane to China, and he begins his journey to save the world.

Chapter 2: The Infiltration

Alex arrives in China and checks into a hotel in Beijing. He spends the next few days meeting with Chinese businessmen and investors. He makes a good impression, and he is invited to a high-level conference on nuclear weapons.

The conference is held at a luxurious resort in the mountains. Alex meets with key Chinese officials and learns more about the new weapon that they are developing. He also meets with Chinese scientists and engineers, and he learns that they are working on a new type of nuclear weapon that is much more powerful than anything that has been created before.

Alex knows that he must stop the Chinese government from developing this new weapon, but he also knows that he needs more information. He decides to go undercover and work as a scientist at the Chinese nuclear weapons facility.

Alex gets a job at the facility under the name of "Dr. Zhang." He works hard and quickly gains the trust of his colleagues. He learns a lot about the new weapon, and he also learns about the security measures that are in place to protect it.

One day, Alex makes a startling discovery. He learns that the Chinese government is planning to use the new weapon to attack the United States. Alex knows that he must stop them, but he also knows that he is in danger.

Alex escapes from the Chinese nuclear weapons facility with the plans for the new weapon. He then makes his way back to the United States, where he delivers the plans to the CIA.

The CIA is grateful for Alex's help. They know that he has saved the world from a terrible threat. Alex is a hero, and he is celebrated for his bravery and his ingenuity.

Chapter 3: The Discovery

Alex has been working undercover at the Chinese nuclear weapons facility for several months. He has learned a lot about the new weapon, and he has also gained the trust of his colleagues.

One day, Alex is working in the lab when he overhears two scientists talking. They are discussing the plans for the new weapon, and they mention that it is designed to be used against the United States.

Alex is shocked. He knows that he must stop the Chinese government from developing this weapon, but he also knows that he is in danger. He could be arrested or even killed if he is caught.

Alex decides to take a risk. He sneaks into the office of the head scientist and steals the plans for the new weapon. He then makes his escape from the facility.

Alex knows that he must get the plans back to the CIA as soon as possible. He boards a plane to the United States, and he delivers the plans to the CIA headquarters.

The CIA is grateful for Alex's help. They know that he has stopped the Chinese government from developing a dangerous new weapon. Alex is a hero, and he is celebrated for his bravery and his ingenuity.

However, Alex's mission is not over. The Chinese government is still a threat, and Alex knows that they will not give up easily. He is determined to continue his work as a spy and to protect the world from danger.

Chapter 4: The Chase

Alex knows that the Chinese government will not take kindly to him stealing the plans for their new weapon. He is sure that they will send agents after him, and he is determined to stay ahead of them.

Alex boards a plane to the United States, but he is not safe yet. The Chinese agents are already on his trail. They track him to the airport, and they try to stop him from boarding the plane.

Alex is able to evade the Chinese agents and board the plane. He takes a seat in the back of the plane, and he watches as the Chinese agents search the other passengers.

The plane takes off, and Alex knows that he is safe for now. But he also knows that the Chinese agents will not give up. They will be waiting for him when he lands in the United States.

Alex arrives in the United States, and he is met by a team of CIA agents. They take him to a safe house, where he can rest and recover.

The CIA knows that the Chinese agents are still a threat, and they want to keep Alex safe. They plan to move him to a different safe house, but Alex insists on staying in the United States. He knows that he needs to stop the Chinese government from getting the plans for the new weapon.

Alex leaves the safe house and goes into hiding. He changes his appearance and uses a fake identity. He knows that the Chinese agents are looking for him, but he is determined to stay one step ahead of them.

Alex begins to track down the Chinese agents who are after him. He follows them to their safe houses, and he listens in on their conversations. He learns that they are planning to attack the CIA headquarters in Langley, Virginia.

Alex knows that he must stop the Chinese agents before they can attack the CIA headquarters. He gathers a team of CIA agents, and they launch a raid on the Chinese safe houses.

The raid is a success. The CIA agents are able to capture the Chinese agents and prevent them from attacking the CIA headquarters. Alex is a hero, and he is celebrated for his bravery and his ingenuity.

The Chinese government is furious that Alex has thwarted their plans. They vow to get revenge, but Alex is ready for them. He knows that the war between the United States and China is not over, and he is determined to protect the world from danger.

Chapter 5: The Rescue

The Chinese government is not giving up. They are still determined to get the plans for the new weapon, and they are not afraid to use force.

Alex knows that he is in danger. The Chinese government has sent their best agents after him, and they will stop at nothing to get the plans back.

One day, Alex is attacked by a team of Chinese agents. He is outnumbered and outgunned, but he is able to fight them off. He escapes, but he knows that the Chinese agents will be back.

Alex goes into hiding, but he cannot stay hidden forever. The Chinese agents will eventually find him, and he will need to be ready for them.

Alex begins to train for the inevitable battle with the Chinese agents. He trains in martial arts, weapons, and stealth. He also learns about the Chinese government's tactics and strategies.

Alex knows that he will need all of his skills and resources to defeat the Chinese agents. He is determined to protect the world from the Chinese government's dangerous new weapon, and he is not going to give up without a fight.

One day, Alex receives a message from the Chinese government. They offer him a deal. If he gives them the plans for the new weapon, they will spare his life.

Alex knows that the Chinese government cannot be trusted. They will not keep their word, and they will kill him anyway. He refuses to give them the plans, and he tells them that he will never stop fighting them.

The Chinese government is furious. They vow to destroy Alex, and they send their most elite agents after him.

Alex is ready for them. He has been training for this moment, and he is determined to defeat the Chinese agents. He fights them off, one by one, and he eventually emerges victorious.

Alex has saved the world from the Chinese government's dangerous new weapon. He is a hero, and he is celebrated for his bravery and his ingenuity.

The Chinese government is defeated, but they are not gone. They will be back, and Alex knows that he will need to be ready for them. But for now, he can rest easy knowing that he has saved the world.

STORY -II
The Robbery

Chapter 1: The Robbery

Jack, the thief, was a master of disguise. He could change his appearance at will, and he was always one step ahead of the police.

One day, Jack decided to rob a bank. He disguised himself as a security guard and walked into the bank. He pulled out a gun and demanded money from the teller.

The teller gave Jack the money, and he quickly left the bank. The police were called, but Jack had already disappeared.

Chapter 2: The Investigation

Detective Smith was assigned to investigate the robbery. He knew that Jack was a dangerous criminal, and he was determined to catch him.

Detective Smith interviewed the witnesses and reviewed the security footage from the bank. He was able to identify Jack, but he still didn't know where he was.

Chapter 3: The Stakeout

Detective Smith put a team of officers on stakeout at the bank. He knew that Jack would strike again soon, and he wanted to be ready for him.

Sure enough, Jack showed up at the bank a few days later. He was disguised as a homeless man, but Detective Smith and his team recognized him.

Chapter 4: The Arrest

The police moved in and arrested Jack. He was taken to jail, where he is awaiting trial.

Jack is now facing a long prison sentence. He has finally been caught, and he will no longer be able to terrorize the city.

Chapter 5: The Aftermath

Detective Smith and his team are heroes. They have put a dangerous criminal behind bars, and they have made the city a safer place.

The people of the city are grateful to Detective Smith and his team for their hard work. They know that they can sleep soundly at night knowing that Jack is of f the streets.

I hope you enjoyed this thief and police story!

Chapter 1: The Robbery

It was a bright and sunny day in the city of Los Angeles. The streets were bustling with activity, and the sun was shining brightly.

Jack, the thief, was walking down the street. He was dressed in a black suit and tie, and he had a briefcase in his hand. He looked like any other businessman on his way to work.

But Jack was not a businessman. He was a thief, and he was on his way to rob a bank.

Jack walked into the bank and approached the teller. He pulled out a gun and demanded money. The teller was terrified, but she gave Jack the money.

Jack quickly left the bank with the money. He got into his car and drove away.

The police were called, but they were unable to catch Jack. He had disappeared into the crowd.

Jack was a master of disguise. He could change his appearance at will, and he was always one step ahead of the police.

The police knew that Jack was a dangerous criminal, and they were determined to catch him. But they were also frustrated. They had been chasing Jack for months, but he had always managed to slip away.

The police knew that Jack would strike again soon. They were determined to be ready for him.

I

hope this is more detailed!

Chapter 2: The Investigation

Detective Smith was assigned to investigate the robbery. He knew that Jack was a dangerous criminal, and he was determined to catch him. Detective Smith interviewed the witnesses and reviewed the security footage from the bank. He was able to identify Jack, but he still didn't know where he was.

The security footage showed Jack entering the bank and approaching the teller. He was wearing a black suit and tie, and he had a briefcase in his hand. He looked like any other businessman on his way to work.

But the footage also showed Jack changing his appearance. He disguised himself as a security guard, a homeless man, and even a woman. He was able to change his appearance so quickly that the witnesses were unable to identify him.

Detective Smith knew that Jack was a master of disguise. He would need to be very careful if he wanted to catch him.

Detective Smith put together a team of officers to help him with the investigation. They interviewed more witnesses and searched for any clues that Jack might have left behind.

After a few days, Detective Smith's team was able to find a lead. They found a parking ticket that Jack had left at the bank. The parking ticket had Jack's real name on it, and it also had his license plate number.

Detective Smith was able to track down Jack's car. He found the car parked in an alleyway. The car was empty, but Detective Smith was able to find a few fingerprints inside the car.

The fingerprints matched Jack's fingerprints. Detective Smith knew that he had finally found Jack's trail.

Detective Smith put out an all-points bulletin for Jack. He also started staking out Jack's known hangouts.

Detective Smith knew that Jack would strike again soon. He was determined to be ready for him.

Chapter 3: The Stakeout

Detective Smith put a team of officers on stakeout at the bank that Jack had robbed. He knew that Jack would strike again soon, and he wanted to be ready for him.

The officers staked out the bank for days, but Jack never showed up. Detective Smith was starting to think that he had lost Jack's trail.

But then, one day, the officers saw a man walking down the street who looked like Jack. The man was dressed in a black suit and tie, and he had a briefcase in his hand. He looked like any other businessman on his way to work.

The officers followed the man to the bank. They watched him go inside, and they waited for him to come out.

A few minutes later, the man came out of the bank. He was carrying a bag full of money. The officers knew that it was Jack.

The officers moved in and arrested Jack. He was taken to jail, where he is awaiting trial.

Jack is now facing a long prison sentence. He has finally been caught, and he will no longer be able to terrorize the city.

Detective Smith and his team are heroes. They have put a dangerous criminal behind bars, and they have made the city a safer place.

The people of the city are grateful to Detective Smith and his team for their hard work. They know that they can sleep soundly at night knowing that Jack is off the streets.

Chapter 4: The Arrest

The officers moved in and arrested Jack. He was carrying a bag full of money. The officers knew that it was Jack.

"You're under arrest," Detective Smith said.

Jack tried to run, but the officers were too fast for him. They tackled him to the ground and handcuffed him.

"I didn't do anything," Jack said. "You've got the wrong guy."

"We know who you are, Jack," Detective Smith said. "We've been watching you for weeks."

The officers took Jack to the police station. He was booked and fingerprinted. He was then taken to a holding cell to await his arraignment.

Jack was charged with robbery, grand theft, and impersonating a police officer. He could face up to 20 years in prison.

Jack's lawyer tried to get him released on bail, but the judge denied the request. He said that Jack was a flight risk and that he was a danger to the community.

Jack is now being held in jail without bail. He is scheduled to go to trial in a few months.

Detective Smith and his team are confident that they will win the case against Jack. They have a strong case against him, and they know that the jury will find him guilty.

Jack is facing a long prison sentence, but he deserves it. He is a dangerous criminal who has terrorized the city for too long. He is finally off the streets, and the people of the city can sleep soundly at night knowing that he is behind bars.

Chapter 5: The Aftermath

Jack is now facing a long prison sentence, but he deserves it. He is a dangerous criminal who has terrorized the city for too long. He is finally off the streets, and the people of the city can sleep soundly at night knowing that he is behind bars.

Detective Smith and his team are heroes. They have put a dangerous criminal behind bars, and they have made the city a safer place.

The people of the city are grateful to Detective Smith and his team for their hard work. They know that they can sleep soundly at night knowing that Jack is off the streets.

The arrest of Jack is a victory for the city, but it is also a reminder that crime is still a problem. The police are working hard to keep the city safe, but they need the help of the community.

If you see something, say something. If you suspect that someone is up to no good, call the police. The police need your help to keep the city safe.

The arrest of Jack is a step in the right direction, but it is not the end of the story. The police will continue to work hard to keep the city safe. And the people of the city can play a role by being vigilant and reporting suspicious activity to the police.

STORY -III
Jack and the Sarah

Chapter 1: The Meet-Cute

It was a cold and rainy night in London. The streets were deserted, and the only sound was the howling wind.

A young woman named Sarah was walking home from work when she saw a man standing in the shadows. He was tall and handsome, with dark hair and blue eyes.

The man smiled at Sarah, and she smiled back. They started talking, and they quickly found out that they had a lot in common.

They both loved to read, they both enjoyed going to the movies, and they both had a passion for travel.

They talked for hours that night, and by the time they parted ways, they were both smitten.

Chapter 2: The Date

The next day, the man called Sarah and asked her out on a date. She said yes, and they went to see a movie together.

They had a great time, and they started dating regularly.

Sarah was falling in love with the man, but she didn't know his name. He always met her in the shadows, and he never told her anything about himself.

Sarah started to get suspicious. She wondered if the man was hiding something from her.

Chapter 3: The Confession

One night, the man finally told Sarah his name. He said his name was Jack, and he was a spy.

Sarah was shocked. She couldn't believe that the man she was falling in love with was a spy.

Jack told Sarah that he had been assigned to infiltrate a crime ring. He said that he needed her help to catch the criminals.

Sarah was scared, but she agreed to help Jack. She knew that she loved him, and she wanted to help him catch the criminals.

Chapter 4: The Heist

Jack and Sarah worked together to plan a heist. They knew that the criminals were planning to rob a bank, and they decided to stop them.

On the night of the heist, Jack and Sarah went to the bank. They disguised themselves as security guards, and they waited for the criminals to arrive.

The criminals arrived at the bank, and they started to rob it. Jack and Sarah intervened, and they fought the criminals.

The criminals were outnumbered, and they were eventually defeated. Jack and Sarah caught the criminals, and they saved the day.

Chapter 5: The Arrest

The criminals were arrested, and they were taken to jail. Jack and Sarah were heroes, and they were celebrated by the city.

Jack and Sarah continued to date, and they eventually got married. They had two children, and they lived happily ever after.

But Jack's work as a spy was not over. He continued to work undercover, and he helped to catch many more criminals.

Sarah was always by Jack's side, and she supported him in his work. She knew that he was a good man, and she was proud of him for what he did.

Jack and Sarah's story is a story of love, romance, crime, spy, and arrest. It is a story about two people who were willing to risk everything to fight for what they believed in. It is a story about the power of love, and the importance of fighting for justice.

Chapter 1: The Meet-Cute

It was a cold and rainy night in London. The streets were deserted, and the only sound was the howling wind.

A young woman named Sarah was walking home from work when she saw a man standing in the shadows. He was tall and handsome, with dark hair and blue eyes.

The man smiled at Sarah, and she smiled back. They started talking, and they quickly found out that they had a lot in common.

They both loved to read, they both enjoyed going to the movies, and they both had a passion for travel.

They talked for hours that night, and by the time they parted ways, they were both smitten.

Sarah couldn't stop thinking about the man. She wanted to see him again, but she didn't know how to contact him.

The next day, Sarah went back to the spot where she had met the man. She stood in the shadows, hoping that he would come back.

After a few hours, the man finally showed up. He smiled when he saw Sarah, and they started talking again.

Sarah told the man that she wanted to see him again. The man said that he would like that too.

They exchanged numbers, and they made plans to go on a date the following weekend.

Sarah was so excited. She couldn't believe that she had met such a wonderful man. She knew that she was going to fall in love with him.

Here are some additional details about the characters and the plot:

- Sarah is a young woman in her early twenties. She is smart, independent, and passionate. She loves to read, travel, and experience new things.
- Jack is a spy in his late twenties. He is handsome, charming, and mysterious. He is also very good at his job.

- The meet-cute happens on a cold and rainy night in London. Sarah is walking home from work when she sees Jack standing in the shadows. They start talking, and they quickly find out that they have a lot in common.
- Sarah is initially suspicious of Jack. She doesn't know who he is or what he wants. But as they get to know each other, she starts to fall in love with him.
- Jack is also falling in love with Sarah. But he knows that he can't tell her his true identity. He is a spy, and he is sworn to secrecy.
- The meet-cute is the beginning of a love story that is full of suspense, danger, and romance. Sarah and Jack will have to overcome many obstacles if they want to be together. But they are both determined to make it work.

Chapter 2: The Date

Sarah was so excited for her date with Jack. She had been looking forward to it all week.

Jack picked Sarah up at her apartment on time. He was dressed in a nice suit, and he looked very handsome.

Sarah was wearing a pretty dress, and she had her hair done. She wanted to look her best for Jack.

They went to a nice restaurant for dinner. They had a great time talking and laughing.

After dinner, they went for a walk in the park. It was a beautiful night, and the stars were out.

They talked for hours, and Sarah felt like she had known Jack for her whole life.

She was falling in love with him, and she knew that he was falling in love with her too.

At the end of the night, Jack walked Sarah to her door. He kissed her goodnight, and she knew that she would never forget this night.

Here are some additional details about the characters and the plot:

- Sarah is nervous but excited for her date with Jack. She wants to make a good impression, and she is hoping that they will have a great time together.
- Jack is also nervous about the date. He doesn't want to say or do anything to scare Sarah away. He knows that she is a special woman, and he wants to make sure that he treats her right.
- The date goes well. Sarah and Jack have a lot in common, and they enjoy each other's company. They laugh and talk for hours, and they feel a connection that they have never felt before.
- By the end of the night, Sarah and Jack are both falling in love. They know that they want to see each other again, and they can't wait for their next date.

- The date is the beginning of a beautiful love story. Sarah and Jack will face many challenges together, but they will always be there for each other. They are soulmates, and they are meant to be together.

Chapter 3: The Confession

Jack and Sarah had been dating for a few months, and they were both falling in love. But Jack knew that he couldn't keep his secret from Sarah any longer. He had to tell her the truth about who he was.

One night, Jack and Sarah were sitting on the couch watching a movie. Jack took a deep breath and said, "Sarah, there's something I need to tell you."

Sarah looked at Jack, and she could tell that he was serious. "What is it?" she asked.

Jack took her hand. "I'm a spy," he said.

Sarah was shocked. She couldn't believe what she was hearing. "A spy?" she asked.

"Yes," Jack said. "I work for MI6."

Sarah didn't know what to say. She was still processing the information.

"I know this is a lot to take in," Jack said. "But I had to tell you the truth. I can't keep it from you anymore."

Sarah took a few minutes to think. She knew that Jack was a good man, and she loved him. She also knew that he was doing important work.

"I understand," she said. "I'm still in shock, but I love you. And I'll support you no matter what."

Jack smiled. "Thank you," he said. "I love you too."

Jack and Sarah's relationship was tested by Jack's secret, but it only made them stronger. They knew that they could trust each other, no matter what. And they knew that they would always be there for each other.

Here are some additional details about the characters and the plot:

- Jack is struggling with whether or not to tell Sarah the truth about his identity. He knows that it will change their relationship, but he also knows that he can't keep it from her any longer.

- Sarah is shocked when Jack tells her the truth. She doesn't know what to think or how to react. But she eventually comes to terms with it, and she supports Jack no matter what.

- The confession is a turning point in Jack and Sarah's relationship. It tests their trust and their love, but it also makes them stronger. They realize that they can face anything together, as long as they have each other.

- The confession is also the beginning of a new chapter in Jack and Sarah's lives. Jack will continue to work as a spy, but he will also have Sarah by his side. They will face many challenges together, but they will always be there for each other. They are soulmates, and they are meant to be together.

Chapter 4: The Heist

Jack and Sarah were working together to stop a crime ring. The crime ring was planning to rob a bank, and Jack and Sarah knew that they had to stop them.

Jack and Sarah came up with a plan. They would disguise themselves as security guards and infiltrate the bank. Once they were inside, they would stop the criminals from robbing the bank.

On the night of the heist, Jack and Sarah put their plan into action. They disguised themselves as security guards and went to the bank.

The criminals were already inside the bank. They were armed and dangerous, but Jack and Sarah were ready for them.

Jack and Sarah fought the criminals, and they were able to stop them from robbing the bank. The criminals were arrested, and the day was saved.

Jack and Sarah were heroes. They were celebrated by the city, and they were given medals for their bravery.

Jack and Sarah were also closer than ever. They had faced danger together, and they had come out stronger. They knew that they could face anything together, as long as they had each other.

Here are some additional details about the characters and the plot:

- Jack and Sarah are working together to stop a crime ring. They are both brave and resourceful, and they are determined to stop the criminals.
- The crime ring is planning to rob a bank. They are armed and dangerous, but Jack and Sarah are ready for them.
- Jack and Sarah disguise themselves as security guards and infiltrate the bank. They are able to stop the criminals from robbing the bank, and they are hailed as heroes.
- The heist is a turning point in Jack and Sarah's relationship. They have faced danger together, and they have come out

stronger. They know that they can face anything together, as long as they have each other.

- The heist is also a victory for good over evil. The criminals are arrested, and the day is saved. Jack and Sarah are heroes, and they are celebrated by the city.

I hope you enjoyed this chapter!

Chapter 5: The Arrest

The criminals were arrested, and they were taken to jail. Jack and Sarah were heroes, and they were celebrated by the city.

Jack and Sarah continued to date, and they eventually got married. They had two children, and they lived happily ever after.

But Jack's work as a spy was not over. He continued to work undercover, and he helped to catch many more criminals.

Sarah was always by Jack's side, and she supported him in his work. She knew that he was a good man, and she was proud of him for what he did.

Jack and Sarah's story is a story of love, romance, crime, spy, and arrest. It is a story about two people who were willing to risk everything to fight for what they believed in. It is a story about the power of love, and the importance of fighting for justice.

Here are some additional details about the characters and the plot:

- Jack and Sarah continued to work together to fight crime. They were both dedicated to their work, and they were always willing to put their lives on the line to protect the innocent.
- Jack and Sarah got married and had two children. They were a happy family, and they loved each other very much.
- Jack continued to work as a spy, and he helped to catch many more criminals. He was a good man, and he was always willing to do what was right.
- Sarah was always by Jack's side, and she supported him in his work. She was a strong woman, and she was always there for Jack, no matter what.
- Jack and Sarah's story is a story of hope and redemption. It is a story about how love can conquer all, even the darkest of evils. It is a story that will stay with you long after you finish reading it.

I hope you enjoyed this chapter!

STORY -IV

Robin,Queen & the Robbers

Here is the story of the queen captive by robber and Robin releasing her from the captivity in 5 chapters:

Chapter 1: The Kidnapping

The year is 1300. The place is England. The king and queen are away on a hunting trip, and the castle is under the care of the captain of the guard. But one night, a group of robbers led by a man named Rober attack the castle and kidnap the queen.

The king and queen are devastated when they hear the news. They offer a reward for the safe return of the queen, but no one comes forward.

Meanwhile, Rober and his men keep the queen captive in a secret dungeon. They treat her well, but she is still a prisoner.

Chapter 2: The Rescue

One day, a young man named Robin Hood hears about the queen's kidnapping. He is a skilled archer and a master of disguise. He decides to rescue the queen himself.

Robin Hood disguises himself as a priest and goes to the castle. He sneaks into the dungeon and finds the queen. He tells her that he is there to rescue her.

The queen is overjoyed. She has been praying for someone to save her. She follows Robin Hood out of the dungeon and they escape from the castle.

Rober and his men are furious when they realize that the queen has escaped. They chase after Robin Hood and the queen, but they are no match for Robin's skills.

Chapter 3: The Chase

Robin Hood and the queen make it to the forest. Rober and his men are close behind, but Robin Hood knows the forest well. He leads the queen through the trees, and Rober and his men are unable to follow.

Robin Hood and the queen eventually come to a river. They have to cross the river to safety, but it is too wide to swim across. Robin Hood builds a raft, and they use the raft to cross the river.

Rober and his men are still on the other side of the river. They are furious, but they know that they cannot cross the river. Robin Hood and the queen have escaped.

Chapter 4: The Reunion

Robin Hood and the queen make it to safety. They are reunited with the king and queen, and they are hailed as heroes.

The king and queen are so grateful to Robin Hood for rescuing the queen. They give him a reward and make him an advisor to the king.

Robin Hood uses his position to help the poor and the oppressed. He becomes a legend, and his stories are told for generations to come.

Chapter 5: The Legacy

The queen's kidnapping is a dark chapter in English history. But it is also a story of hope and redemption. It is a story about how one man can make a difference, and how love can conquer all.

Robin Hood's legacy lives on today. He is a symbol of hope and justice, and his stories continue to inspire people all over the world.

Chapter 1: The Kidnapping

The year is 1300. The place is England. The king and queen are away on a hunting trip, and the castle is under the care of the captain of the guard. But one night, a group of robbers led by a man named Rober attack the castle and kidnap the queen.

The king and queen are devastated when they hear the news. They offer a reward for the safe return of the queen, but no one comes forward.

Meanwhile, Rober and his men keep the queen captive in a secret dungeon. They treat her well, but she is still a prisoner.

Here are some additional details about the characters and the plot:

- The king and queen are a kind and benevolent couple who are loved by their subjects.
- Rober is a ruthless robber who is willing to do anything to get what he wants.
- The captain of the guard is a loyal and dedicated servant to the king and queen, but he is no match for Rober's men.
- The queen is a beautiful and intelligent woman who is also a skilled archer.

The kidnapping is a dark day for England. The king and queen are beloved by their subjects, and their kidnapping is a sign that the country is in danger. Rober is a ruthless and dangerous man, and his actions threaten the peace of the kingdom.

The queen's kidnapping is also a personal tragedy for the king and queen. They are deeply in love, and they are devastated to be separated. The queen is also worried about her children, who are still young.

The kidnapping is a turning point in the story. It sets in motion a chain of events that will lead to Robin Hood's rescue of the queen. It also shows the dark side of human nature, and the lengths that people will go to for power and wealth.

Chapter 2: The Rescue

One day, a young man named Robin Hood hears about the queen's kidnapping. He is a skilled archer and a master of disguise. He decides to rescue the queen himself.

Robin Hood disguises himself as a priest and goes to the castle. He sneaks into the dungeon and finds the queen. He tells her that he is there to rescue her.

The queen is overjoyed. She has been praying for someone to save her. She follows Robin Hood out of the dungeon and they escape from the castle.

Rober and his men are furious when they realize that the queen has escaped. They chase after Robin Hood and the queen, but they are no match for Robin's skills.

Here are some additional details about the characters and the plot:

- Robin Hood is a legendary outlaw who is known for his bravery and his Robin Hood-mask. He is a skilled archer and a master of disguise. He is also a kind and compassionate man who is willing to help those in need.
- The queen is grateful to Robin Hood for rescuing her. She is also impressed by his skills and his courage. She begins to develop feelings for Robin Hood, and he for her.
- Rober and his men are determined to capture Robin Hood and the queen. They are willing to do anything to get what they want, even if it means killing them.

The rescue is a daring and dangerous mission. Robin Hood must use all of his skills and cunning to escape from the castle and the queen's captors. He must also protect the queen from harm.

The rescue is a success. Robin Hood and the queen escape from the castle and the queen's captors. They are reunited with the king and queen, and they are hailed as heroes.

The rescue is a turning point in the story. It shows Robin Hood's bravery and his skills. It also shows the queen's courage and her determination. The rescue also brings Robin Hood and the queen closer together, and it sets in motion a chain of events that will change their lives forever.

Chapter 3: The Chase

Robin Hood and the queen make it to the forest. Rober and his men are close behind, but Robin Hood knows the forest well. He leads the queen through the trees, and Rober and his men are unable to follow.

Robin Hood and the queen eventually come to a river. They have to cross the river to safety, but it is too wide to swim across. Robin Hood builds a raft, and they use the raft to cross the river.

Rober and his men are still on the other side of the river. They are furious, but they know that they cannot cross the river. Robin Hood and the queen have escaped.

Here are some additional details about the characters and the plot:

- The forest is a dangerous place, but it is also a place where Robin Hood is at his best. He knows the forest like the back of his hand, and he is able to use the trees and the bushes to hide from Rober and his men.
- The queen is scared, but she trusts Robin Hood. She knows that he will protect her, and she follows his lead.
- Rober and his men are frustrated. They are close to catching Robin Hood and the queen, but they cannot seem to catch them. They are also starting to lose hope.

The chase is a thrilling and suspenseful sequence. It shows Robin Hood's skills as a tracker and a woodsman. It also shows the queen's courage and her determination. The chase also brings Robin Hood and the queen closer together, and it sets in motion a chain of events that will change their lives forever.

The chase ends with Robin Hood and the queen safely crossing the river. Rober and his men are left behind, defeated. Robin Hood and the queen have escaped, and they are one step closer to freedom.

Chapter 4: The Reunion

Robin Hood and the queen make it to safety. They are reunited with the king and queen, and they are hailed as heroes.

The king and queen are so grateful to Robin Hood for rescuing the queen. They give him a reward and make him an advisor to the king.

Robin Hood uses his position to help the poor and the oppressed. He becomes a legend, and his stories are told for generations to come.

Here are some additional details about the characters and the plot:

- The king and queen are overjoyed to be reunited with their daughter. They are also grateful to Robin Hood for his help.
- Robin Hood is honored to be made an advisor to the king. He uses his position to help the poor and the oppressed. He also becomes a friend and confidant to the king.
- The queen is grateful to Robin Hood for rescuing her. She also develops feelings for him, and he for her. They eventually get married and have a family.

The reunion is a happy and joyous occasion. It is a celebration of love, courage, and hope. It is also a reminder that even in the darkest of times, there is always hope for a better future.

The reunion is a turning point in the story. It sets in motion a chain of events that will change the course of history. Robin Hood becomes a powerful advisor to the king, and he uses his position to help the poor and the oppressed. He also becomes a legend, and his stories are told for generations to come.

The reunion is also a personal triumph for Robin Hood and the queen. They have overcome great challenges, and they have found love and happiness together. They are an inspiration to everyone who knows them, and they show that anything is possible if you have the courage to believe in yourself.

Chapter 5: The Legacy

Robin Hood's legacy lives on today. He is a symbol of hope and justice, and his stories continue to inspire people all over the world.

Robin Hood is remembered as a hero who fought for the poor and the oppressed. He is also remembered as a man of love and compassion. His stories are told to children to teach them about the importance of standing up for what is right, even when it is difficult.

Robin Hood's legacy is a reminder that even in the darkest of times, there is always hope for a better future. It is also a reminder that we should all strive to be like Robin Hood: a person who fights for what is right, no matter what the cost.

Here are some additional details about the characters and the plot:

- Robin Hood's legacy is a powerful one. It inspires people to fight for justice and equality. It also reminds us that we should never give up hope, no matter how difficult things may seem.
- The queen's legacy is also one of hope and courage. She is a reminder that even in the face of adversity, women can be strong and independent. She is also a symbol of hope for all women who have ever been oppressed.
- Rober's legacy is one of greed and corruption. He is a reminder that there are people in the world who will do anything to get what they want, even if it means hurting others. He is also a cautionary tale about the dangers of power and wealth.

The legacy of Robin Hood, the queen, and Rober is a complex one. It is a story of love, courage, hope, greed, corruption, and power. It is a story that has been told and retold for centuries, and it is a story that will continue to be told for generations to come.

The stories of Robin Hood, the queen, and Rober are timeless tales of love, courage, hope, greed, corruption, and power. They have been told and retold for centuries, and they continue to inspire people all over the world.

In these stories, we meet a cast of unforgettable characters: Robin Hood, the heroic outlaw who fights for the poor and the oppressed; the queen, a strong and independent woman who is kidnapped by Rober; and Rober, a ruthless and greedy man who will stop at nothing to get what he wants.

Together, these characters embark on a journey of love, loss, and redemption. They face challenges and obstacles, but they never give up hope. They teach us about the importance of standing up for what is right, even when it is difficult. They remind us that even in the darkest of times, there is always hope for a better future.

These stories are more than just entertainment. They are parables about the human condition. They teach us about the importance of love, courage, hope, and justice. They remind us that we should never give up on our dreams, no matter how difficult things may seem.

STORY -V
The Danger
of
Interest

The Dangers of Interest

Chapter 1: The Loan

The year is 2042, and the world is in chaos. The climate has changed drastically, and natural disasters are a regular occurrence. In this time of crisis, a young couple named Anya and Ben are struggling to keep their business afloat.

Anya and Ben run a small bakery in a small town. They make fresh bread and pastries, and they sell them to the local community. However, the business is struggling. The cost of ingredients has gone up, and people are less willing to spend money on luxuries like fresh bread.

One day, Anya and Ben are approached by a banker named Shylock. Shylock offers to lend them money to help their business. However, he charges them a very high interest rate. Anya and Ben are hesitant to agree to the terms, but they feel like they have no choice.

Chapter 2: The Interest

Anya and Ben take out the loan, and they use the money to buy more ingredients and to hire more staff. The business starts to do better, but they are still struggling to make ends meet. The interest payments are taking a big bite out of their profits, and they are starting to fall behind on their payments.

Shylock is relentless. He comes to collect the interest payments every month, and he always demands more money. Anya and Ben are starting to feel like they are drowning in debt. They don't know how they are going to keep up with the payments.

Chapter 3: The Boycott

One day, Anya has an idea. She goes to the local library and does some research on interest. She learns that interest is a form of debt that can be harmful to society. It can lead to inequality, poverty, and even violence.

Anya decides to take a stand against interest. She goes to the town hall and gives a speech about the dangers of interest. She calls on the townspeople to boycott Shylock's bank. The townspeople are inspired by Anya's speech, and they agree to boycott the bank.

Shylock is furious. He tries to sue Anya for defamation, but the case is dismissed. The townspeople have spoken, and they are no longer willing to support Shylock's business. Shylock is forced to close his bank, and Anya and Ben are able to save their business.

Chapter 4: The Aftermath

The boycott of Shylock's bank is a success. The townspeople are now aware of the dangers of interest, and they are no longer willing to support businesses that charge high interest rates. This leads to a decrease in the amount of debt in the community, and it helps to create a more equitable society.

Anya and Ben are able to save their business, and they are able to continue to provide fresh bread and pastries to the local community. They are grateful for the support of the townspeople, and they are committed to fighting against the dangers of interest.

Chapter 5: The Future

The story ends with a message of hope. Anya and Ben's story shows that it is possible to fight against the dangers of interest and to create a more equitable society. It is a reminder that we should all be aware of the dangers of debt, and that we should stand up for what we believe in, even if it means going against the status quo.

This story is a cautionary tale about the dangers of interest. It shows how interest can be used to exploit people and to control them. It is a reminder that we should be careful about the kind of debt that we take on, and that we should fight against systems that use interest to harm people.

Chapter 1: The Loan:

The year is 2042, and the world is in chaos. The climate has changed drastically, and natural disasters are a regular occurrence. In this time of crisis, a young couple named Anya and Ben are struggling to keep their business afloat.

Anya and Ben run a small bakery in a small town. They make fresh bread and pastries, and they sell them to the local community. However, the business is struggling. The cost of ingredients has gone up, and people are less willing to spend money on luxuries like fresh bread.

One day, Anya and Ben are approached by a banker named Shylock. Shylock offers to lend them money to help their business. However, he charges them a very high interest rate. Anya and Ben are hesitant to agree to the terms, but they feel like they have no choice.

"We're desperate," Anya says. "We can't afford to lose our business."

"I understand," Shylock says. "But I can't give you a loan without interest. That's how banks make money."

Anya and Ben look at each other. They know that Shylock is right. They need the money, even if it means paying high interest rates.

"We'll take it," Ben says.

Shylock smiles. "Excellent. I'll draw up the paperwork."

Anya and Ben sign the paperwork, and they leave Shylock's office with a sense of relief. They have the money they need to save their business.

However, they also know that they are now in debt to Shylock. They will have to pay back the loan with interest, and that will be a challenge. But they are determined to make it work. They are not going to let Shylock win.

Anya and Ben go back to their bakery and start working harder than ever. They make more bread and pastries, and they sell them at a lower price. They also start a delivery service to reach more customers.

The business starts to improve, and Anya and Ben are able to make the loan payments. However, it is still a struggle. They are working long hours, and they are barely making enough money to cover their expenses.

One day, Shylock comes to collect the interest payments. He is not happy with the amount of money that Anya and Ben have paid him.

"You're behind on your payments," he says. "You need to pay me more money."

"We can't afford to pay you more," Ben says. "We're barely making enough money to cover our expenses."

"That's not my problem," Shylock says. "You signed the contract, and now you have to pay me."

Anya and Ben are furious. They feel like Shylock is taking advantage of them. But they know that they have no choice but to pay him.

They hand over the money, and Shylock leaves. Anya and Ben are left feeling defeated. They know that they are in a difficult situation, but they are determined to fight back. They will not let Shylock win.

This is just the beginning of Anya and Ben's fight against Shylock and the dangers of interest. In the next chapters, they will learn more about the dangers of interest, and they will take action to fight against it. They will inspire others to do the same, and they will ultimately succeed in creating a more equitable society.

Chapter 2: The Interest:

Anya and Ben are struggling to keep up with the interest payments on their loan. The interest rate is so high that they are barely making enough money to cover their expenses.

They are working long hours, and they are exhausted. They are also starting to argue more, and they are feeling stressed and overwhelmed.

One day, Anya comes home from work and finds Ben sitting at the kitchen table. He is looking at the loan paperwork, and he is frowning.

"I've been doing some research," he says. "And I've learned that interest is a form of debt that can be harmful to society."

Anya is surprised. "What do you mean?" she asks.

"I mean that interest can lead to inequality, poverty, and even violence," Ben says. "It can make it difficult for people to get out of debt, and it can trap them in a cycle of poverty."

Anya is starting to understand. "So, you're saying that interest is bad?" she asks.

"Yes," Ben says. "I think it's a system that is designed to keep people down."

Anya is silent for a moment. She is thinking about what Ben has said. She knows that he is right. Interest can be a very harmful thing.

"I think we need to do something about it," she says.

Ben nods. "I agree," he says. "We need to fight back against interest and to create a more equitable society."

Anya and Ben decide to take action. They start by talking to their friends and family about the dangers of interest. They also start a blog and a social media campaign to raise awareness of the issue.

Their efforts start to gain traction. More and more people are learning about the dangers of interest, and they are starting to demand change.

Anya and Ben are inspired by the response they are getting. They know that they are making a difference, and they are determined to keep fighting.

They know that it will be a long and difficult battle, but they are not giving up. They believe that a more equitable society is possible, and they are committed to creating it.

This is just the beginning of Anya and Ben's fight against interest. In the next chapters, they will continue to raise awareness of the issue, and they will take more action to fight back. They will inspire others to do the same, and they will ultimately succeed in creating a more equitable society.

Chapter 3: The Boycott:

Anya and Ben's efforts to raise awareness of the dangers of interest are starting to pay off. More and more people are learning about the issue, and they are starting to demand change.

One day, Anya and Ben are approached by a group of activists who are organizing a boycott of Shylock's bank. They ask Anya and Ben to speak at the boycott rally.

Anya and Ben are hesitant at first. They are worried about the potential backlash from Shylock. But they know that they need to do something to fight back against interest.

They agree to speak at the rally, and they deliver a powerful speech about the dangers of interest. They call on the people of the town to boycott Shylock's bank and to create a more equitable society.

The rally is a success. Hundreds of people attend, and they are inspired by Anya and Ben's speech. They agree to boycott Shylock's bank, and they pledge to fight against interest.

Shylock is furious when he learns about the boycott. He tries to intimidate Anya and Ben, but they refuse to back down. They know that they are doing the right thing, and they are determined to keep fighting.

The boycott continues for several weeks. More and more people join the boycott, and Shylock's bank starts to lose business. He is forced to lower his interest rates, and he eventually closes the bank.

Anya and Ben are victorious. They have helped to create a more equitable society, and they have shown that it is possible to fight back against interest.

This is just one example of how people can fight back against interest. There are many other ways to do it, and we all have a role to play. We can talk to our friends and family about the dangers of interest. We can support businesses that do not charge interest. We can vote for politicians who are committed to fighting against interest.

We can all make a difference. We can create a more equitable society, and we can stop interest from harming people.

Chapter 4: The Aftermath:

The boycott of Shylock's bank is a success. The bank is forced to close, and interest rates in the town are lowered. Anya and Ben are hailed as heroes, and they are now able to run their bakery without the burden of debt.

The success of the boycott inspires others to fight back against interest. People all over the country start to boycott banks that charge high interest rates. Interest rates start to fall, and people are able to get out of debt more easily.

The fight against interest is not over. There are still many banks that charge high interest rates, and there are still many people who are struggling with debt. But the boycott of Shylock's bank is a sign of hope. It shows that people can make a difference, and it shows that it is possible to create a more equitable society.

Anya and Ben continue to fight against interest. They speak at rallies, they write articles, and they work with politicians to change the laws. They are determined to create a world where everyone has a fair chance, and where interest is no longer a barrier to success.

They know that it will be a long and difficult battle, but they are not giving up. They believe that a more equitable society is possible, and they are committed to creating it.

The story of Anya and Ben is a story of hope. It is a story about the power of people to make a difference. It is a story about the importance of fighting for what we believe in.

It is a story that we can all learn from. We all have a role to play in creating a more equitable society. We can all fight against interest, and we can all make a difference.

Chapter 5: The Future:

Anya and Ben's fight against interest continues for many years. They speak at rallies, they write articles, and they work with politicians to change the laws. They are determined to create a world where everyone has a fair chance, and where interest is no longer a barrier to success.

They eventually succeed in their mission. Interest rates are lowered across the country, and people are able to get out of debt more easily. Anya and Ben are hailed as heroes, and they are remembered for their role in creating a more equitable society.

The future is bright for Anya and Ben. They are able to continue running their bakery, and they are able to help others who are struggling with debt. They are also able to start a family, and they raise their children to believe in the power of fighting for what you believe in.

The story of Anya and Ben is a story of hope. It is a story about the power of people to make a difference. It is a story about the importance of fighting for what we believe in.

It is a story that we can all learn from. We all have a role to play in creating a more equitable society. We can all fight against interest, and we can all make a difference.

Here are some specific examples of how the future could be different if interest did not exist:

- People would be able to start businesses and pursue their dreams without having to worry about debt.
- People would be able to save for retirement and for their children's education without having to worry about interest rates.
- People would be able to afford to buy homes and cars without having to take out loans.
- People would be less likely to fall into poverty and homelessness.
- The economy would be more stable and prosperous.

In short, a world without interest would be a more just and equitable world. It would be a world where everyone has a fair chance to succeed, regardless of their background or circumstances.

STORY -VI
The Kingdom
of
Intrestia

Chapter 1: The Kingdom of Interestia

Once upon a time, there was a kingdom called Interestia. It was a prosperous kingdom, with a strong economy and a happy population. However, the kingdom was built on interest, and the people were slowly becoming enslaved to debt.

The king of Interestia was a greedy man. He loved money more than anything else in the world. He charged high interest rates on loans, and he made sure that the people of his kingdom were always in debt.

The people of Interestia were starting to suffer. They were working long hours to pay off their debts, and they had no time for their families or their hobbies. They were also becoming more and more divided, as the rich got richer and the poor got poorer.

Chapter 2: Anya's Awakening

One day, a young woman named Anya decided to do something about it. She was tired of seeing her people suffer. She was tired of seeing the rich get richer and the poor get poorer. She was tired of living in a kingdom that was built on interest.

Anya started a movement to abolish interest in Interestia. She traveled all over the kingdom, speaking to people about the dangers of interest. She also started a petition to the king, demanding that he end the practice of charging interest.

Chapter 3: The King's Wrath

The king was furious when he heard about Anya's movement. He tried to silence her, but she refused to back down. She continued to speak out against interest, and she continued to gather support for her cause.

The king eventually sent his guards to arrest Anya. She was thrown in prison, and she was threatened with torture. But Anya refused to give up. She continued to fight for her cause, even from behind bars.

Chapter 4: The People Rise Up

The people of Interestia were inspired by Anya's courage. They began to protest against the king and his policies. They demanded that he abolish interest and free Anya from prison.

The king was forced to back down. He agreed to abolish interest in Interestia, and he ordered Anya's release from prison. The people rejoiced, and Anya was hailed as a hero.

Chapter 5: The New Interestia

The end of interest in Interestia was a major turning point for the kingdom. The people were finally free from debt, and they were able to start building a more equitable society. The economy also improved, as people were able to invest their money in productive activities instead of paying interest.

Anya's story is a reminder that interest is a destructive force. It creates inequality, poverty, and division. It also stifles economic growth. We need to move away from an interest-based economy and towards a more equitable system where everyone has a chance to succeed.

Chapter 1: The Kingdom of Interestia:

Once upon a time, there was a kingdom called Interestia. It was a prosperous kingdom, with a strong economy and a happy population. The people of Interestia were known for their hard work and their ingenuity. They were also known for their love of money.

The king of Interestia was a greedy man. He loved money more than anything else in the world. He charged high interest rates on loans, and he made sure that the people of his kingdom were always in debt.

The people of Interestia were starting to suffer. They were working long hours to pay off their debts, and they had no time for their families or their hobbies. They were also becoming more and more divided, as the rich got richer and the poor got poorer.

The king was happy with the situation. He was making more money than ever before, and he didn't care about the suffering of his people. He thought that they were weak and lazy, and he didn't deserve to be free from debt.

One day, a young woman named Anya decided to do something about it. She was tired of seeing her people suffer. She was tired of seeing the rich get richer and the poor get poorer. She was tired of living in a kingdom that was built on interest.

Anya started a movement to abolish interest in Interestia. She traveled all over the kingdom, speaking to people about the dangers of interest. She also started a petition to the king, demanding that he end the practice of charging interest.

The people of Interestia were inspired by Anya's courage. They began to protest against the king and his policies. They demanded that he abolish interest and free Anya from prison.

The king was forced to back down. He agreed to abolish interest in Interestia, and he ordered Anya's release from prison. The people rejoiced, and Anya was hailed as a hero.

The end of interest in Interestia was a major turning point for the kingdom. The people were finally free from debt, and they were able to start building a more equitable society. The economy also improved, as people were able to invest their money in productive activities instead of paying interest.

Anya's story is a reminder that interest is a destructive force. It creates inequality, poverty, and division. It also stifles economic growth. We need to move away from an interest-based economy and towards a more equitable system where everyone has a chance to succeed.

Here are some specific examples of the problems caused by interest in Interestia:

- **Debt:** The people of Interestia were constantly in debt. They borrowed money from the king and his allies at high interest rates, and they were never able to pay it back. This led to poverty, hunger, and homelessness.
- **Inequality:** The rich got richer and the poor got poorer. The rich could afford to borrow money at low interest rates, while the poor were often forced to borrow money at high interest rates. This created a cycle of poverty that was difficult to break.
- **Instability:** The economy of Interestia was volatile and unpredictable. Changes in interest rates could have a major impact on the economy, leading to recessions and financial crises.
- **Unfairness:** Interest was a form of exploitation. The people of Interestia were essentially paying the king and his allies for the privilege of using their own money. This was a very unfair system, especially for those who were already struggling financially.

The story of Interestia is a cautionary tale about the dangers of interest-based economy. It shows how interest can lead to poverty, inequality, instability, and unfairness. We need to move away from an interest-based economy and towards a more equitable system where everyone has a chance to succeed.

Chapter 2: Anya's Awakening:

Anya was a young woman who lived in the kingdom of Interestia. She was a kind and compassionate person, but she was also very intelligent and perceptive. She saw the problems caused by interest, and she knew that something had to be done.

One day, Anya was walking through the market when she saw a poor woman crying. The woman had borrowed money from the king at a high interest rate, and she was now unable to pay it back. She was going to be forced to sell her home and her belongings, and she didn't know what she was going to do.

Anya was heartbroken by the woman's story. She knew that this was just one example of the many people who were suffering because of interest. She decided that she had to do something to help.

Anya started a movement to abolish interest in Interestia. She traveled all over the kingdom, speaking to people about the dangers of interest. She also started a petition to the king, demanding that he end the practice of charging interest.

The people of Interestia were inspired by Anya's courage. They began to protest against the king and his policies. They demanded that he abolish interest and free Anya from prison.

The king was furious when he heard about Anya's movement. He tried to silence her, but she refused to back down. She continued to speak out against interest, and she continued to gather support for her cause.

The king eventually sent his guards to arrest Anya. She was thrown in prison, and she was threatened with torture. But Anya refused to give up. She continued to fight for her cause, even from behind bars.

Anya's imprisonment only served to galvanize the people of Interestia. They were even more determined to abolish interest now that they saw how the king was willing to silence their dissent.

The people of Interestia continued to protest, and they continued to demand that the king abolish interest. The king was eventually forced to back down. He agreed to abolish interest in Interestia, and he ordered Anya's release from prison.

The people rejoiced, and Anya was hailed as a hero. She had saved the people of Interestia from the tyranny of interest.

Anya's awakening was a turning point for the kingdom of Interestia. The people were finally free from debt, and they were able to start building a more equitable society. The economy also improved, as people were able to invest their money in productive activities instead of paying interest.

Anya's story is a reminder that we all have the power to make a difference. We can stand up to injustice, and we can fight for what we believe in. We can create a better world, one where everyone has a chance to succeed.

Chapter 3: The King's Wrath:

The king was furious when he heard about Anya's movement. He had been charging interest on loans for years, and he had made a lot of money from it. He didn't want to give up that income, and he didn't want to lose control over the people of Interestia.

The king sent his guards to arrest Anya. They found her speaking to a crowd of people about the dangers of interest. The guards tried to silence her, but she refused to back down. She continued to speak out against interest, even in the face of danger.

The king was even more furious when he heard about this. He ordered the guards to throw Anya in prison. They put her in a dark cell, and they threatened to torture her if she didn't stop talking about interest.

Anya was scared, but she refused to give up. She knew that she was fighting for a just cause, and she was determined to see it through. She continued to speak out against interest, even from behind bars.

The king's wrath only served to galvanize the people of Interestia. They were even more determined to abolish interest now that they saw how the king was willing to silence their dissent.

The people of Interestia continued to protest, and they continued to demand that the king abolish interest. The king was eventually forced to back down. He agreed to abolish interest in Interestia, and he ordered Anya's release from prison.

The people rejoiced, and Anya was hailed as a hero. She had saved the people of Interestia from the tyranny of interest.

The king was forced to accept his defeat, but he was not happy about it. He vowed to get revenge on Anya someday.

Anya was aware of the king's threat, but she was not afraid. She knew that she had done the right thing, and she was confident that she would be able to defend herself if the king ever tried to harm her.

The story of Anya and the king is a cautionary tale about the dangers of power. It shows how power can corrupt, and how it can be used to oppress the people. It also shows how important it is to stand up to injustice, even when it is dangerous to do so.

Chapter 4: The People Rise Up:

The people of Interestia were inspired by Anya's courage. They saw how she had stood up to the king and his guards, and they were determined to do the same.

They began to protest against the king and his policies. They demanded that he abolish interest and free Anya from prison.

The protests grew larger and larger. People from all over the kingdom came together to demand change. The king was forced to respond.

He tried to silence the protesters with threats and violence, but they would not back down. They continued to speak out against interest, and they continued to demand change.

The king eventually realized that he could not defeat the people on his own. He agreed to abolish interest in Interestia, and he ordered Anya's release from prison.

The people rejoiced, and Anya was hailed as a hero. She had saved the people of Interestia from the tyranny of interest.

The end of interest in Interestia was a major turning point for the kingdom. The people were finally free from debt, and they were able to start building a more equitable society. The economy also improved, as people were able to invest their money in productive activities instead of paying interest.

The story of the people of Interestia is a reminder that we all have the power to make a difference. We can stand up to injustice, and we can fight for what we believe in. We can create a better world, one where everyone has a chance to succeed.

Here are some specific examples of how the people of Interestia rose up against the king:

- They organized protests and demonstrations.
- They boycotted the king's businesses.
- They spread awareness of the dangers of interest.
- They refused to pay interest on their loans.

The people of Interestia were united in their goal of abolishing interest. They were willing to make sacrifices and to take risks in order to achieve their goal. They were an inspiration to people all over the world, and they showed that even a small group of people can make a big difference.

Chapter 5: The New Interestia:

The new Interestia was a much better place than the old Interestia. The people were free from debt, and they were able to live their lives without fear of poverty or exploitation. The economy was also stronger, as people were able to invest their money in productive activities.

Anya was a national hero. She was celebrated for her courage and her determination to fight for what she believed in. She had shown the world that even a single person can make a difference.

Here are some specific examples of the positive changes that occurred after interest was abolished in Interestia:

- **Debt:** The people of Interestia were finally free from debt. They were no longer trapped in a cycle of poverty and exploitation. They were able to invest their money in their businesses and their communities, and they were able to build a better future for themselves and their families.
- **Inequality:** The gap between the rich and the poor was reduced. Everyone had a fair chance to succeed, regardless of their social class.
- **Instability:** The economy of Interestia became more stable. There were no more recessions or financial crises.
- **Fairness:** The people of Interestia were no longer exploited by the wealthy. They were able to keep the fruits of their labor, and they were able to build a more equitable society.

The story of Interestia is a cautionary tale about the dangers of interest-based economy. It shows how interest can lead to poverty, inequality, instability, and unfairness. We need to move away from an interest-based economy and towards a more equitable system where everyone has a chance to succeed.

The new Interestia was a model for other kingdoms. People from all over the world came to see how Interestia had abolished interest and created a more equitable society. The story of Interestia inspired people to fight for change in their own kingdoms.

The new Interestia was a symbol of hope for the future. It showed that it was possible to create a better world, one where everyone had a chance to succeed.

- **The power of unity:** The people of Interestia were able to achieve great things because they were united in their goal of abolishing interest. They were willing to make sacrifices and to take risks in order to achieve their goal. This shows the power of unity and cooperation.
- **The importance of fighting for what you believe in:** Anya fought for what she believed in, even when it was dangerous to do so. She was willing to put her life on the line for the cause of abolishing interest. This shows the importance of fighting for what you believe in, even when it is difficult.
- **The importance of hope:** The people of Interestia never gave up hope, even when the odds were stacked against them. They believed that it was possible to create a better world, one where everyone had a chance to succeed. This shows the importance of hope and perseverance.

The story of the new Interestia is a reminder that we can all create a better world, one where everyone has a chance to succeed. We need to be united in our goals, we need to fight for what we believe in, and we need to never give up hope.

some additional details to the above story:

- The kingdom of Interestia was a fictional kingdom, but it was inspired by real events. In many parts of the world, people are still trapped in a cycle of poverty because of interest.
- The character of Anya was a fictional character, but she was inspired by real-life activists who have fought against the injustice of interest.
- The story of the kingdom of Interestia is a cautionary tale about the dangers of interest. It shows how interest can lead to poverty, inequality, and unfairness. It also shows how we can create a better world by working together and fighting for what we believe in.

Here are some specific examples of how interest can lead to poverty, inequality, and unfairness:

- **Poverty:** When people are forced to borrow money at high interest rates, they often end up in debt. This can make it difficult for them to make ends meet, and they may eventually have to sell their possessions or even their homes.
- **Inequality:** The wealthy can afford to borrow money at low interest rates, while the poor are often forced to borrow money at high interest rates. This gives the wealthy an unfair advantage, and it helps to create a cycle of poverty.
- **Unfairness:** Interest is a form of exploitation. It allows the wealthy to profit from the misfortune of others. This is unfair to the poor, who are often the ones who are most affected by interest.

The story of the kingdom of Interestia is a call to action for us to fight against the injustice of interest and to create a more equitable world for everyone. We can do this by:

- Educating ourselves about the dangers of interest.
- Supporting organizations that are working to abolish interest.
- Making changes in our own lives by refusing to borrow money at high interest rates and by supporting businesses that are committed to ethical practices.

Together, we can create a better world, one where everyone has a chance to succeed.

- The concept of interest has been around for centuries. It was first introduced in ancient Babylonia, and it has been used in many different cultures and societies ever since.
- Interest is a form of rent. It is the price that borrowers pay to lenders for the use of their money.
- Interest rates can vary depending on a number of factors, including the risk of the borrower defaulting on the loan, the length of the loan, and the prevailing market conditions.
- Interest can be a major burden for borrowers, especially those who are already struggling to make ends meet. It can lead to debt, poverty, and inequality.
- There are a number of alternatives to interest, such as microfinance and Islamic finance. These alternatives can help to reduce the burden of debt and create a more equitable financial system.

Here are some specific examples of alternatives to interest:

- **Microfinance:** Microfinance is a type of lending that provides small loans to low-income borrowers. Microfinance loans are often used to start businesses or to cover basic expenses.
- **Islamic finance:** Islamic finance is a financial system that is based on Islamic law. Islamic law prohibits interest, so Islamic financial institutions use a variety of alternative methods to finance transaction

here are some more information about the above result:

- **The abolition of interest:** The abolition of interest was a major step towards creating a more equitable economy in Interestia. It meant that borrowers could now borrow money without having to worry about being trapped in a cycle of debt. This was especially beneficial for the poor, who were often the ones who were most affected by interest.

- **The creation of new financial institutions:** The creation of new financial institutions that did not charge interest was another important step in creating a more equitable economy. These institutions provided loans to borrowers at a fair rate, and they did not profit from the misfortune of others. This helped to level the playing field for borrowers and to reduce the gap between the rich and the poor.
- **Investment in education and job training programs:** The investment in education and job training programs helped to create a more skilled workforce in Interestia. This led to increased economic growth and job opportunities for everyone. It also helped to reduce poverty, as people were now better equipped to find good jobs and earn a decent living.
- **The provision of social safety nets:** The provision of social safety nets for the poor and the vulnerable helped to ensure that everyone had a basic standard of living. This included things like food stamps, housing assistance, and healthcare. These programs helped to lift people out of poverty and to give them a chance to improve their lives.

The changes that were made in Interestia after the abolition of interest had a profound impact on the country. The economy grew, poverty decreased, and the people were happier and more prosperous. The kingdom became a model for other countries, and it showed the world that an interest-free economy is possible.

The story of Interestia is a reminder that we can create a better world by working together and fighting for what we believe in. We can create an economy that is fair and equitable, where everyone has a chance to succeed.

- **The abolition of interest led to a decrease in the cost of borrowing money.** This made it easier for people to start businesses and to invest in their education and training.
- **The creation of new financial institutions led to an increase in competition in the financial sector.** This resulted in lower interest rates and better customer service for borrowers.
- **The investment in education and job training programs led to an increase in the number of skilled workers in Interestia.** This made the country more attractive to businesses and led to increased economic growth.
- **The provision of social safety nets helped to reduce poverty and inequality in Interestia.** This made the country a more equitable place to live.

The abolition of interest had a number of positive consequences for the kingdom of Interestia. It led to a decrease in the cost of borrowing money, an increase in competition in the financial sector, an increase in the number of skilled workers, and a reduction in poverty and inequality. These changes made Interestia a more prosperous and equitable place to live.

The story of Interestia is a reminder that we can create a better world by working together and fighting for what we believe in. We can create an economy that is fair and equitable, where everyone has a chance to succeed.

Here are some additional thoughts on the abolition of interest:

- The abolition of interest would be a major change to the current financial system. It would require a significant shift in the way that we think about money and lending.
- However, there are a number of potential benefits to abolishing interest. It could lead to a more equitable economy, where everyone has a fair chance to succeed. It could also help to

reduce poverty and inequality.

- There are also some challenges that would need to be addressed if interest were to be abolished. For example, it would be important to ensure that there is still a way for businesses to get the capital they need to grow.

- Overall, the abolition of interest is a complex issue with both potential benefits and challenges. It is something that we should continue to explore and debate as we work to create a more equitable and sustainable economy.

SHORT STORIES

The Fortune Teller's Curse

Once upon a time, there was a young man named Eric who lived in a small town. He was kind and intelligent, but he was also very poor. His father was an alcoholic who gambled away all of their money, and his mother had died when he was young.

One day, Eric met a beautiful young woman named Sarah. Sarah was also from a poor family, but she was very ambitious. She dreamed of becoming a famous actress, and she was willing to do whatever it took to achieve her dreams.

Eric and Sarah fell in love, and they soon got married. They moved to Los Angeles, where Sarah started auditioning for roles. Eric got a job as a waiter to support them, but it was hard to make ends meet.

Sarah eventually got a break and landed a role in a small movie. She was thrilled, but the excitement was short-lived. The movie was a flop, and Sarah was blacklisted by Hollywood.

Eric and Sarah were devastated. They had lost all of their savings, and they didn't know what to do. Eric started to gamble in an attempt to make money, but he soon lost even more money.

Sarah turned to fortune telling to try to make money. She was good at it, and she soon started to make a good living. However, she became obsessed with fortune telling, and she started to neglect Eric.

Eric was angry and hurt. He felt like Sarah was abandoning him, and he started to drink heavily. He also started to gamble again, and he soon lost everything they had.

Sarah was horrified when she found out about Eric's gambling. She tried to help him, but he refused to stop. He became more and more distant, and he eventually left Sarah.

Sarah was heartbroken. She had lost everything: her husband, her career, and her dreams. She didn't know what to do. She went to see a therapist, who helped her to realize that she needed to take control of her own life.

Sarah got a job as a waitress, and she started to rebuild her life. She also started to write a book about her experiences. The book was a success, and it helped Sarah to heal from her past.

Sarah's story is a cautionary tale about the dangers of alcoholism, gambling, and fortune telling. It shows how these vices can lead to pain, heartbreak, and even crime. It also shows how love, romance, and hope can help us to overcome difficult challenges.

The story also shows how important it is to be independent and to stand up for ourselves. Sarah was able to escape from her addiction and to rebuild her life because she was strong and determined. She didn't let her circumstances control her, and she didn't let her past define her.

Sarah's story is a reminder that we can all overcome difficult challenges if we are willing to fight for what we believe in. We can all create a better future for ourselves, no matter what our circumstances may be.

The Porn Trap: One Man's Journey to Overcome Addiction

Once upon a time, there was a man named John who was addicted to pornography. He would watch it for hours every day, and it began to take over his life. He stopped spending time with his friends and family, and his work performance suffered. He also became more and more isolated, and he started to have trouble sleeping and concentrating.

One day, John's wife found out about his addiction. She was furious, and she told him to get help. John agreed, and he started going to therapy. He also joined a support group for people struggling with pornography addiction.

It was a long and difficult road, but John eventually overcame his addiction. He learned how to control his urges, and he started to rebuild his life. He got back in touch with his friends and family, and his work performance improved. He also started to feel better about himself, and he was able to sleep and concentrate again.

John's story is a reminder of the dangers of pornography addiction. It can ruin relationships, damage careers, and lead to mental health problems. If you or someone you know is struggling with pornography addiction, there is help available. There are many resources available, including therapy, support groups, and online forums. With the right help, you can overcome your addiction and reclaim your life.

Here are some additional details about the ill effects of pornography addiction:

- It can lead to relationship problems. When people are addicted to pornography, they often neglect their partners in favor of watching porn. This can lead to feelings of resentment and distrust in the relationship.
- It can damage careers. People who are addicted to pornography often find it difficult to concentrate at work. They may also be more likely to make mistakes or engage in risky behavior. This can lead to job loss or demotion.

- It can lead to mental health problems. Pornography addiction can contribute to anxiety, depression, and low self-esteem. It can also lead to problems with intimacy and relationships.

If you are struggling with pornography addiction, there is help available. There are many resources available, including therapy, support groups, and online forums. With the right help, you can overcome your addiction and reclaim your life.

The Cigarette That Nearly Killed Me

John was a 30-year-old man who had been smoking cigarettes since he was 16 years old. He started smoking because he thought it was cool, and he quickly became addicted.

At first, John didn't think smoking was a big deal. He could still run and play sports, and he didn't seem to be getting sick any more often than his non-smoking friends. But as the years went by, John started to notice the negative effects of smoking.

He started to cough more often, and he had trouble breathing. He also started to get sick more often, and he had to take more medication. John's doctor told him that he needed to quit smoking, but John didn't think he could do it.

One day, John woke up with a terrible cough. He couldn't breathe, and he felt like he was going to die. He went to the hospital, and the doctors told him that he had pneumonia. John was lucky to be alive, but the doctors told him that he would need to quit smoking if he wanted to stay that way.

John knew that he had to quit smoking, but he didn't know how. He tried to quit on his own, but he couldn't do it. He needed help, so he went to see a therapist. The therapist helped John to understand the reasons why he was smoking, and she gave him tools to help him quit.

It was a long and difficult road, but John eventually quit smoking. He has been smoke-free for 5 years now, and he is much healthier than he was when he was smoking. He can run and play sports again, and he doesn't get sick as often. John is so glad that he quit smoking, and he knows that he made the right decision for his health.

John's story is a reminder of the dangers of cigarette smoking. It can have a devastating impact on your health, and it can even kill you. If you are a smoker, please consider quitting. It is the best thing you can do for your health.

Here are some additional details about the ill effects of cigarette smoking:

- Cigarette smoking is the leading cause of preventable death in the United States.
- Smoking can cause cancer, heart disease, stroke, chronic obstructive pulmonary disease (COPD), and many other health problems.
- Smoking can make you look older than you really are. It can also cause wrinkles, yellow teeth, and gum disease.
- Smoking can be addictive. It can be very difficult to quit smoking on your own.

If you are a smoker, there is help available. There are many resources available, including therapy, support groups, and online forums. With the right help, you can quit smoking and reclaim your life.

The Road to Recovery: One Man's Story of Overcoming Gambling Addiction

The man's name was John, and he was a gambler. He had been gambling since he was a teenager, and he had always been good at it. He had won a lot of money over the years, but he had also lost a lot of money.

John was a high-stakes gambler. He would often bet large sums of money on a single hand of cards or roll of the dice. He knew that he was taking a risk, but he also knew that he could win big.

One day, John was playing poker in a casino. He was winning big, and he was feeling confident. He decided to bet even more money than he normally would. He lost the hand, and he lost a lot of money.

John was furious. He couldn't believe that he had lost so much money. He started to gamble more and more, trying to win back his losses. But the more he gambled, the more he lost.

Soon, John was in debt. He had borrowed money from friends and family, and he was even starting to borrow money from loan sharks. He was desperate to win back his money, but he just kept losing.

John's gambling addiction was ruining his life. He was losing his job, his relationships, and his home. He was even starting to think about suicide.

One day, John woke up and realized that he couldn't go on like this anymore. He needed help. He went to see a therapist, and he started attending Gamblers Anonymous meetings.

It was a long and difficult road, but John eventually got his life back on track. He paid off his debts, he got a new job, and he started rebuilding his relationships. He is now a recovering gambler, and he is determined to never gamble again.

John's story is a reminder of the dangers of gambling addiction. It can ruin lives, and it can even lead to death. If you or someone you know is struggling with gambling addiction, please seek help. There is help available, and you don't have to go through this alone.

Here are some additional details about the story:

- John's gambling addiction started when he was a teenager. He was drawn to the excitement of gambling, and he soon found himself hooked.
- John's gambling addiction caused him a lot of problems in his life. He lost money, he lost relationships, and he even lost his job.
- John eventually got help for his gambling addiction. He went to therapy and started attending Gamblers Anonymous meetings.
- John is now a recovering gambler. He is determined to never gamble again, and he is rebuilding his life.

I hope this story helps to raise awareness of the dangers of gambling addiction. If you or someone you know is struggling with gambling addiction, please seek help. There is help available, and you don't have to go through this alone.

Milton Keynes UK
Ingram Content Group UK Ltd.
UKHW010931280823
427620UK00001B/162